ana &
ANDREW

The New Baby

by Christine Platt
illustrated by Junissa Bianda

Calico Kid

An Imprint of Magic Wagon
abdobooks.com

About the Author
Christine A. Platt is an author and scholar of African and African-American history. A beloved storyteller of the African diaspora, Christine enjoys writing historical fiction and non-fiction for people of all ages. You can learn more about her and her work at christineaplatt.com.

For my favorite midwife, Ebony Marcelle. —CP

To my number one supporter, Krisna Aditya. —JB

abdobooks.com

Published by Magic Wagon, a division of ABDO, PO Box 398166, Minneapolis, Minnesota 55439. Copyright © 2020 by Abdo Consulting Group, Inc. International copyrights reserved in all countries. No part of this book may be reproduced in any form without written permission from the publisher. Calico Kid™ is a trademark and logo of Magic Wagon.

Printed in the United States of America, North Mankato, Minnesota.
102019
012020

 THIS BOOK CONTAINS RECYCLED MATERIALS

Written by Christine Platt
Illustrated by Junissa Bianda
Edited by Tamara L. Britton
Art Directed by Candice Keimig

Library of Congress Control Number: 2019942040

Publisher's Cataloging-in-Publication Data

Names: Platt, Christine, author. I Bianda, Junissa, illustrator.
Title: The new baby / by Christine Platt ; illustrated by Junissa Bianda.
Description: Minneapolis, Minnesota : Magic Wagon, 2020. I Series: Ana & Andrew
Summary: Ana & Andrew are expecting a sibling! The family is very excited. Mama's family arrives from Trinidad, and everyone helps to get ready. When the baby arrives, Ana & Andrew learn from Granny that in African American culture, a baby's name often tells an important story.
Identifiers: ISBN 9781532136382 (lib. bdg.) I ISBN 9781644942628 (pbk.) I ISBN 9781532136986 (ebook) I ISBN 9781532137280 (Read-to-Me ebook)
Subjects: LCSH: African American families--Juvenile fiction. I Infants (Newborn)--Juvenile fiction. I Siblings--Juvenile fiction I Family reunions--Juvenile fiction. I Baby names--Juvenile fiction. I Ancestry--Juvenile fiction.
Classification: DDC [E]--dc23

Table of Contents

Chapter #1
Guess What?

When Ana and Andrew arrived home from school, Mama was taking a nap on the couch. Papa walked over and tucked her in with a soft blanket.

"Mama sure is tired these days," Andrew said.

"Yes," Ana agreed. "She's always sleeping."

Papa smiled. "Mama *is* tired. But there's a good reason why. We'll tell you both after dinner tonight."

Ana and Andrew could not imagine what was making Mama so tired.

"Maybe she's a secret magician," Ana guessed.

"Or maybe she's a spy," Andrew wondered.

They couldn't wait to find out.

After dinner, Mama yawned and Ana asked, "Why are you so tired, Mama?"

"Are you a secret spy?" Andrew asked.

Mama laughed. "I am definitely not a spy."

"Are you a magician?" Ana inquired.

"Most certainly not," Mama laughed again.

Suddenly, Papa came out of the kitchen carrying a big cake with a little rattle on top. "Guess what? Mama is so tired because she's pregnant. We're having a baby!"

"A baby?" Andrew shouted as he did a wiggle dance. "Oh boy!"

"Or it could be, *oh girl*!" Ana giggled.

"We'll just have to wait and see."
Mama smiled and patted her belly.
Ana and Andrew were very excited.
They couldn't wait to meet their
new baby brother or sister.

Chapter #2
A Big Surprise!

Every week, Mama's belly grew larger and rounder. Ana and Andrew marked off each day on the calendar to countdown the arrival of the new baby.

SEPTEMBER

SUN	MON	TUE	WED	THU	FRI	SAT

11

Sometimes, they went with Mama to her checkups to find out how the baby was developing. Mama went to a midwife. "I am going to help with the birth of your new baby brother or sister," Mrs. Marcelle said. "And since your parents have chosen to have a home birth, you'll get to be there."

"Oh boy!" Andrew said.

"Or, oh girl!" Ana giggled. "Sissy and I want a baby sister."

"Well, the gender of the baby will be a surprise for all of us." Papa smiled.

"Ana and Andrew, softly place your hands on your mama's belly," Mrs. Marcelle instructed. As soon as they did, the baby started wiggling.

Andrew said, "Definitely a boy. He dances just like me!" And everyone laughed.

There was a lot to do before the new baby arrived. Papa set up a crib and changing table in the nursery. Andrew organized the gifts they received from family and friends. Ana folded the baby's clothing.

"Everything is so tiny," Ana said. "Just like the clothes that Sissy wears."

Soon, there was only one week left on the calendar. It was almost time for the baby to be born!

On Saturday afternoon, there was a knock at the front door. "Andrew, can you see who has stopped by for a visit?" Papa asked.

"Yes, Papa." Andrew went to the front door. "Who is it?"

"Surprise!" a familiar voice shouted. "What a go on? It's me! Ya cousin, Michael!"

Andrew opened the front door and gave his cousin a big hug. Standing behind Michael were the rest of their family who lived on the island of Trinidad. Uncle Errol had a bouquet of flowers for Mama. Tanty Renee was holding their baby cousin, Amada. And there was even a bigger surprise—Granny, Mama's mother!

"Granny!" Ana and Andrew shouted, hugging her tightly.

"Welcome, family!" Papa smiled.

"You're just in time."

Chapter #3
It's Time

Mrs. Marcelle came over every day to check on Mama's progress. When Ana and Andrew checked off the last day on the calendar, she said, "It's time!"

"Oh boy!" Andrew did a wiggle dance.

"Or, oh girl!" Ana hugged Sissy and crossed her fingers.

While Mrs. Marcelle helped Mama and Papa with the birth, Ana and Andrew waited in the living room with their family.

"I can't wait to find out the baby's name," Ana said excitedly. "Mama and Papa said we won't know until the baby is born."

Grandma smiled. "I love to see your mama and papa honoring our ancestors' naming traditions."

"How so?" Andrew asked.

"Well, many years ago, our ancestors waited to announce the name of a child until he or she was born. The name often told a story—whether the baby was born in the morning or evening. What day he or she was born. Or even reflected the parents' hope for their child's future."

"That's so cool!" Ana said.

"Very cool." Granny smiled. "Your mama's name is Anora, which means grace. And I bet that's why they chose 'Ana' for you. Your name means full of grace."

"What does my name mean?" Andrew asked.

"Andrew means brave," Granny
said. "So, I am sure your new sibling's
name will have a special meaning."

"I can't wait to find out what it is!"
Ana and Andrew said.

"Me either," Granny said. "It's
almost time for us to find out!"

Chapter #4
Meet the Baby

A few hours later, Papa came into the living room and asked, "Is everyone ready to meet the baby?"

"Yes!" they shouted.